MW00947598

This book is dedicated to:

Georgia and Vivienne Wluka;
Daniel, Eli, and Sofi Metz; Greta
Thunberg; Vic Barrett; Xiye
Bastida; Isra Hirsi; Jamie Margolin;
Xiuhtezcatl Martinez; Varshini
Prakash; Alexandria Villaseñor; and
all the other youth who are inspiring
the authors and people everywhere
to protect our planet.

Janelle London and Matthew Metz

illustrated by
Ilya Fortuna

Rory barely had time to pop open his eyes,
when Dad burst through the door with a birthday surprise.

Rory's big sister Tina was quick to arrive.
"Hey Rory," she giggled, "your gift is alive."

Rory ripped off the wrapping, his hands moving fast.
"This is great," he cried out, "a hamster at last!"

"He made a poo!
We should take him outside.
He dove into the towel!
He must like to hide.

Let's find him a tunnel to
hide in and play.
Come on little Sparky,"
said Rory, "this way!"

“Now, where’s a good tunnel?
I hope somewhere near.
Oh look!” exclaimed Rory,
“See what I found here?”

"Rory, no!" Tina cried. "Sparky can't be in there!
The tailpipe is full of black soot and bad air.

The stuff in that tailpipe is much worse than dirt.
Take him out right away, before he gets hurt."

"When cars burn gasoline, what comes out is smoke.
It hurts lungs and brains," Tina said. "It's no joke."

"Don't all cars need gas," Rory asked, "just to run?
Why would they use gas if it hurt anyone?"

"It does," Tina said. "The smoke stays in the air.
Makes some kids get asthma, like our neighbor Claire."

Rory asked, “Where’d you learn all about gasoline?”
Tina said, “Science class with Ms. McGreen.”

“Where does the gasoline come from?” asked Rory.
“Come along,” Tina said, “and I’ll tell you the story.”

400 million years ago

"Deep underground, gasoline starts as oil
from dead plants and dinosaurs, squished in the soil."

"Getting oil out from under the sea takes a rig.
From the shore it looks small, but up close it's so big!

The steel teeth of drill bits chomp at the sea floor.
Then pipes pull the oil out until there's no more."

"Oil's a liquid," said Tina. "It spills and it leaks.
When it does, it sticks to birds' feathers and beaks.

It sticks to a new mama otter's thick fur."
Rory cried, "Then her babies can't cuddle with her!"

Tina said, “Ocean tankers and long pipelines
take the oil on a journey to get it refined.

Refineries send poison out into the air.”
Rory said, “But for people nearby, that’s not fair!”

Oil Refinery

"Refineries boil oil to make gasoline,
which trucks take to gas stations—very unclean!"

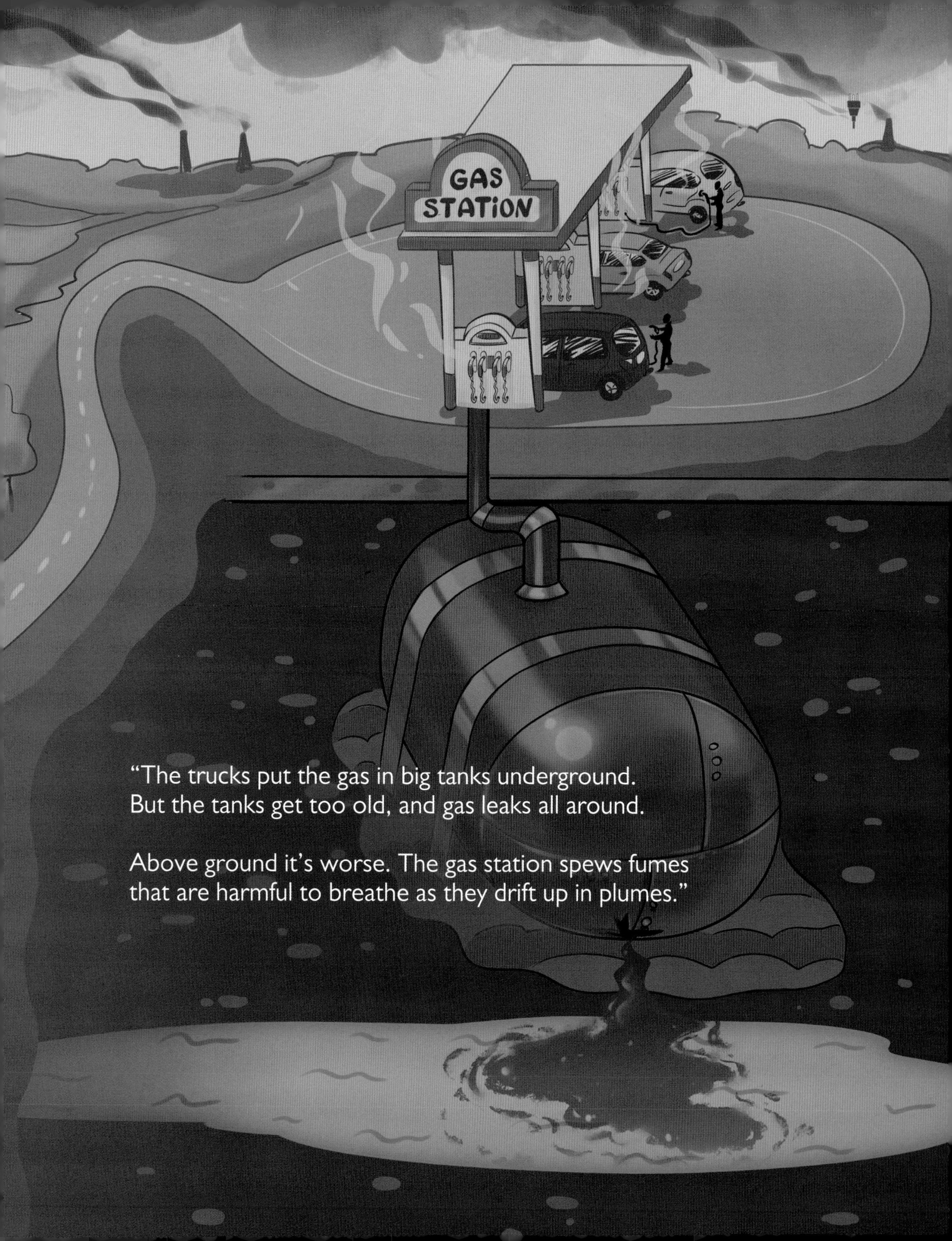

"The trucks put the gas in big tanks underground.
But the tanks get too old, and gas leaks all around.

Above ground it's worse. The gas station spews fumes
that are harmful to breathe as they drift up in plumes."

"And that smoke," Tina said, "that I told you about?
When cars burn gasoline, that's not all that comes out.

Also carbon dioxide—for short, 'CO_2.'
Twenty pounds for each gallon of gas that goes through.

The carbon dioxide's invisible stuff.
In nature, it's fine—the amount's just enough.

It's when *humans* burn fuels that the problems arise,
using way too much carbon to power our rides.

All the extra goes up many thousands of feet.
It thickens the atmosphere; traps the sun's heat."

"The heat causes warming of land and of seas.
It doesn't take much, not too many degrees,

to form a big storm or a fire in the trees."
"A tornado," said Rory, "instead of a breeze!"

Tina said, “Heat melts ice caps and raises the seas,
making people leave home and become refugees.”
Sparky

"The heat makes some places get too hot and dry."
"Without water," said Rory, "the animals could die!"

"Gasoline is so bad! I don't like it one bit!
I wish there were some way to stop using it!"

NO GAS! CLEAN FUTURE!
WE ♥ OUR PLANET
WE ♥ CLEAN AIR
STOP GASOLINE!

“We can stop using gas! We can walk, skip, or run,
or bike, skate, or scoot—much more clean! Much more fun!

We can carpool or ride on the train or the bus.
The less gas we’re using, the better for us.”

"But what if we need to go fast or long-distance?
How can we, without gasoline for assistance?"

Just then, though the day was sunny and bright,
out of nowhere a lightning bolt FLASHED blinding light.

With a big sudden jolt came a thunderclap: BOOM!
And Sparky was gone! Disappeared from the room!

The kids rushed outside, but they didn't go far.
They found Sparky perched on…a whole different car!

"There's no tailpipe!" said Rory. "There's a plug in its place,
and Sparky is sparking—just look at his face!"

"This car is electric," said Tina. "No gas!
We studied these cars in McGreen's science class.

No dirty gas stations, no tailpipe pollution.
Our car problems have an electric solution!"

"Electricity coming from wind and from sun
cuts the carbon dioxide from tons to near none."

Tina said, "Without gas, an electric car's cleaner."
"Now we have one!" said Rory. "A car that is greener!"

"Hey, check it out Dad!" the children both cried.
"Can we try the car please? Can we go for a ride?"

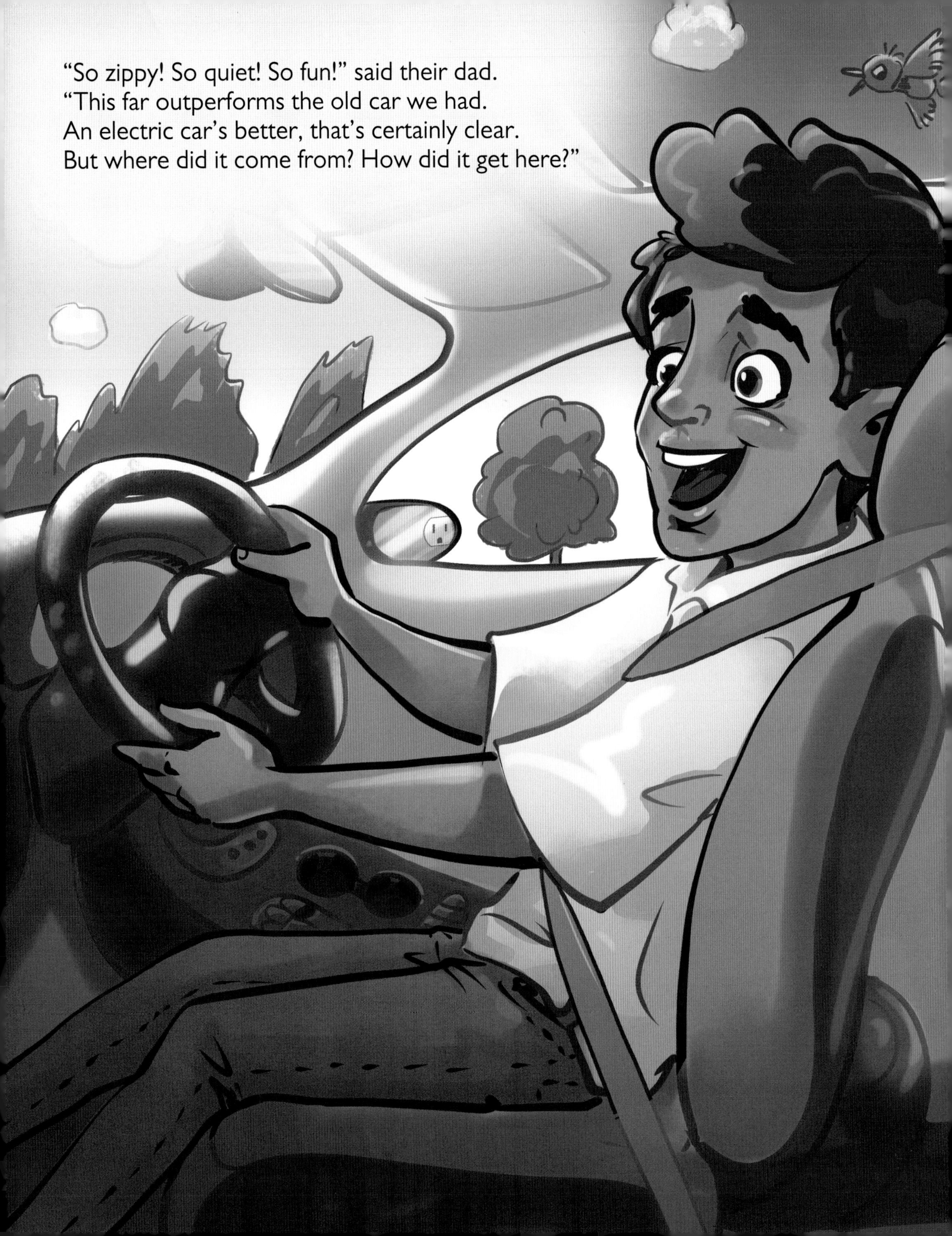

"So zippy! So quiet! So fun!" said their dad.
"This far outperforms the old car we had.
An electric car's better, that's certainly clear.
But where did it come from? How did it get here?"

"Maybe it's magic," a tiny voice sounded.
"Who said that?" asked Dad, looking astounded.

He sat there in silence,
stunned and blinking.
But only the children
could see Sparky winking.

That's the end of this book. There's no more to this story about gasoline, Sparky, and Tina and Rory.

The moral is this: For a planet that's green, we've got to stop using so much gasoline.

To learn how you can help make the switch from gasoline to cleaner alternatives, visit Sparky at coltura.org.

Acknowledgments

The authors are grateful to the many adults and children who reviewed the book and provided helpful suggestions, including: Isaac Morales, Lexi and Gage Lee, Carson and Drew Hilborn, Nathaniel Hannan, Kari and Ashley Trail, Flynn Berns, Sofi Metz, Georgia and Vivienne Wluka, Zoe Hart, Max Castelein, Anushka Srinivasan, June Sobel, Maryann Cocca-Leffler, Andrew Gottlieb, Jordana Wluka-Bishop, Mitch London, Billiam James, Daniel Steinberg, Rusty West, Carlos Manzanedo, Jackie Childress, Stephen Szmed, Rachel Barchus, Franke James, Adrienne Briggs, Dana Doron, Anna Berns, Anisha Mehta, Marie Hurabiell, Kim Leue Bick, Dale Burr, Lydia Smith, Gwyn Morgan, Rachel Szmed, Stacey Meinzen, Tom Stein, Lisa Antillon, Hannah B. Cruz, Christine Arnould, Jodie Spear Goldberg, Greg Pimstone, Garven Garcia, Yadira Morales, and Sheri Brisson.

Coltura is a nonprofit working toward a gasoline-free America. 100% of the proceeds from this book go to our work advancing climate, health, and equity by moving the country from gasoline to cleaner alternatives. Join us at Coltura.org.

www.mascotbooks.com

Sparky's Electrifying Tale

For more information, please contact:
Mascot Books
620 Herndon Parkway, Suite 320
Herndon, VA 20170
info@mascotbooks.com

Library of Congress Control Number: 2020921406

CPSIA Code: PRT0121A
ISBN-13: 978-1-64543-860-1

Printed in the United States